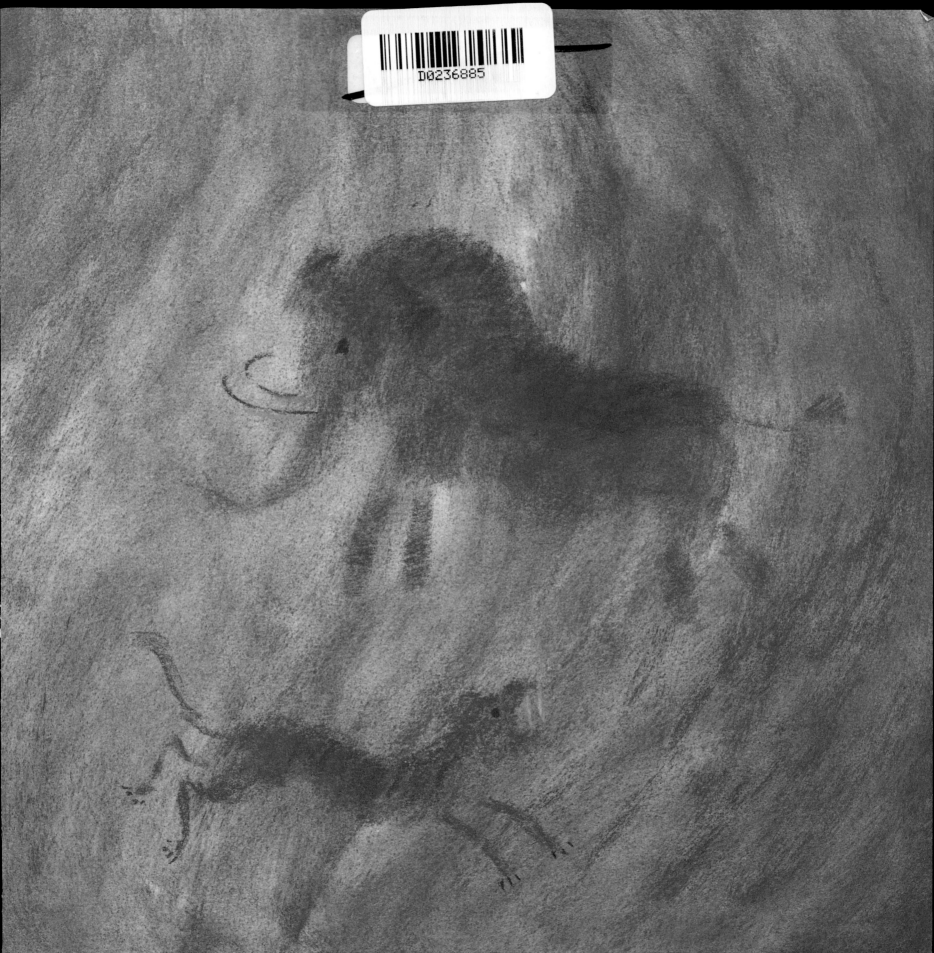

© 2004 The Chicken House

First published in the United Kingdom in 2004 by
The Chicken House, 2 Palmer Street, Frome, Somerset, BA11 1DS

Text and Illustrations © 2004 James Mayhew

Designed by Ian Butterworth

Printed and bound in Singapore

British Library Cataloguing in Publication Data available

ISBN: 1 904442 18 8

To my very own BOY,
with love

BOY

James Mayhew

The Chicken HOUSE

Boy woke up.
It was cold in the cave.
'Where's warm?' said Boy to his Ma and Pa.
'Under the blankets, with us,' they said.

'There's no room for me,'
said Boy. 'Let me have your place.'

'You'll have to share,' said Ma and Pa.
But Boy didn't want to.

Boy went outside and waited for the sun to come up.
'Then it will be warm,' he thought.
But it was cloudy.
Boy felt colder than ever.

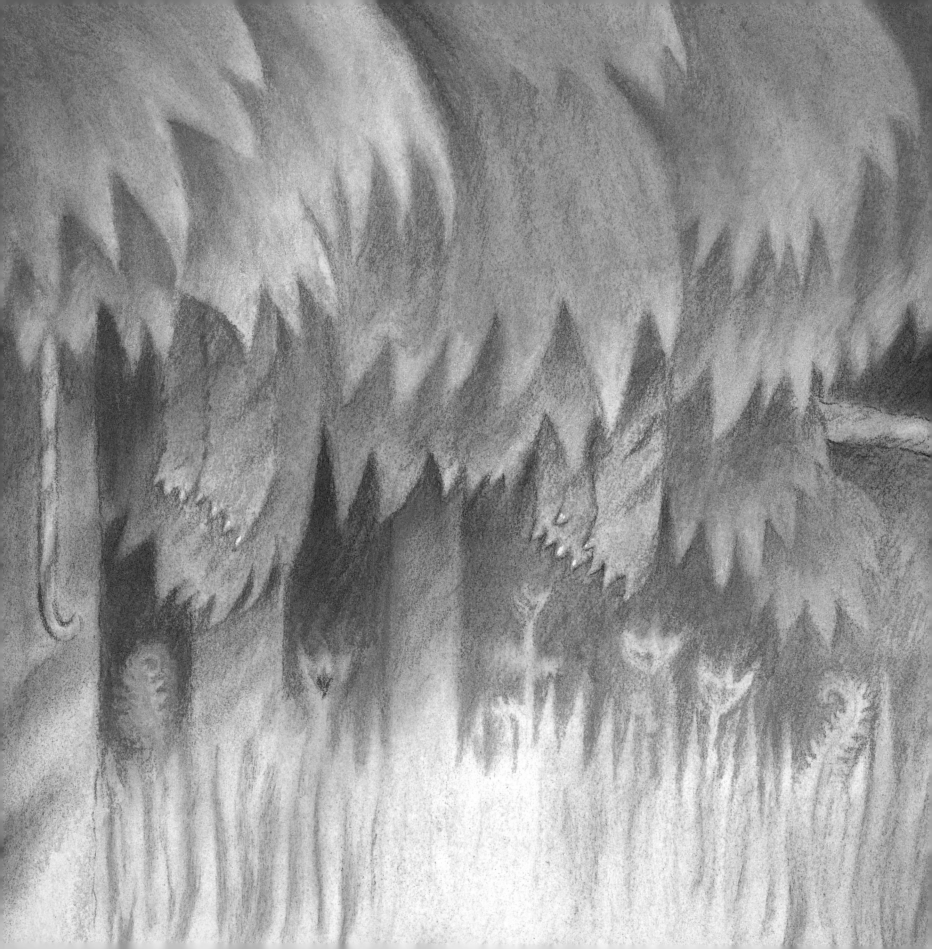

Boy went through the leafy green
forest and sat in a tree.
'Here's warm,' he thought.

'GRRRRRR!'
said a hungry Sabre-Toothed Tiger.
'This is my place, you can't stay here.'

'Why not?' said Boy.

'Because I might eat you up!'
said the Sabre-Toothed Tiger.

Boy didn't like that idea at all,
so he ran off and sat in the long tall grass.
'Here's warm,' he thought.

'Taroooooot!'

said a Woolly Mammoth.
'This is my place,
you can't stay here!'

'Why not?' said Boy.

'Because I might step on you,'
said the Woolly Mammoth.

Boy didn't like that idea at all,
so he ran off and sat down on
a round red rock.
'Here's warm,' he thought.

'YAAAWWWWWN!'

said a sleepy Dinosaur.
'This is my place,
you can't stay here.'

'Why not?' said Boy.

'Because I might roll
over and squash
you!' said the
Dinosaur.

Boy didn't like that idea either,
so he ran over the hill and up a mountain.
'Here's warm,' he thought. 'Here's very warm.'
And he lay down in the sand and fell asleep.

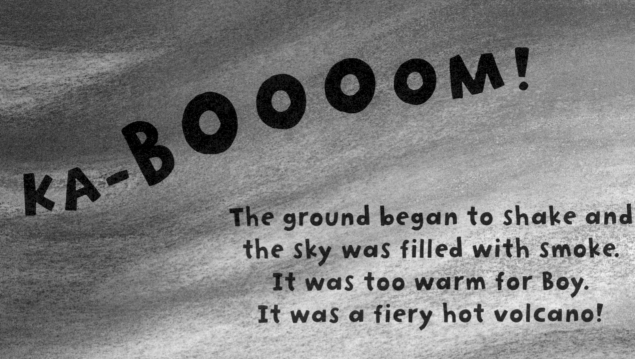

KA-BOOOOM!

The ground began to shake and
the sky was filled with smoke.
It was too warm for Boy.
It was a fiery hot volcano!

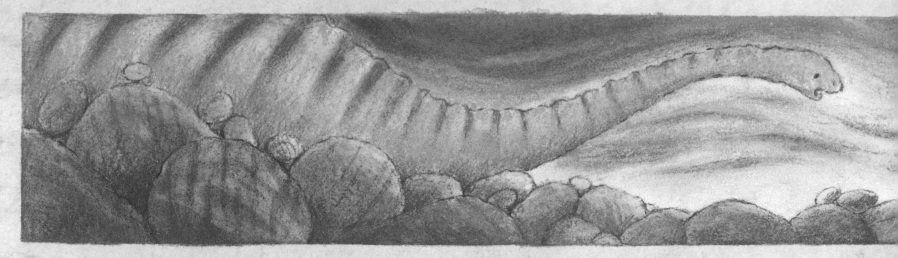

Boy ran back over the round red rocks . . .

back through the long tall grass . . .

back through the leafy green forest . . .

... and into the cold dark cave.

He climbed under the
blanket with Ma and Pa.
'Here's warm,' said Boy.
'Can I share with you?'
'Yes,' said Ma and Pa.

And there was just enough room.